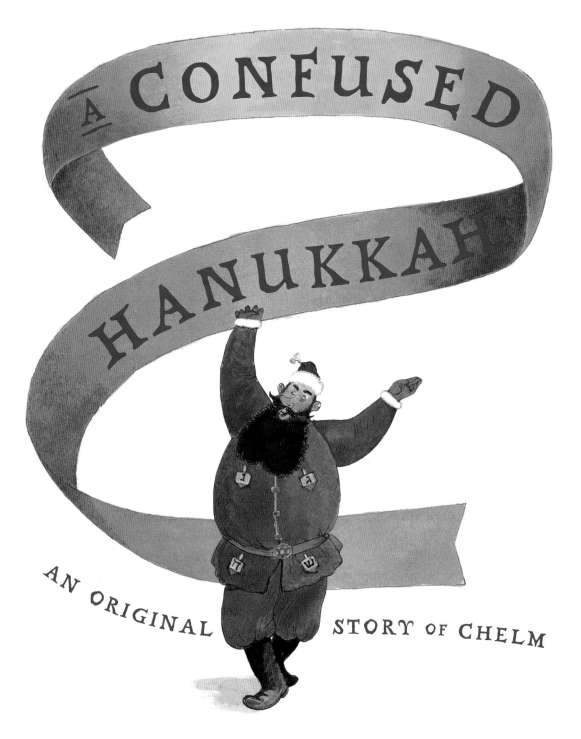

A CONFUSED HANUKKAH

AN ORIGINAL STORY OF CHELM

BY JON KOONS

ILLUSTRATED BY S. D. SCHINDLER

DUTTON CHILDREN'S BOOKS · NEW YORK

Thanks to my folks, Irv and Leah, who introduced me to Chelm; to Don and Pat, who
pointed me to the right guy; and to the right guy, Steve Meltzer, editor extraordinaire,
whose patience and creativity helped me turn a good little story into a great little storybook
J.K.

———

Library of Congress Cataloging-in-Publication Data

Koons, Jon.
A confused Hanukkah: an original story of Chelm/by Jon Koons;
illustrated by S. D. Schindler.—1st ed.
p. cm.
Summary: The villagers of Chelm, in the rabbi's absence,
send a messenger to a nearby village in order to be reminded
how to prepare for the coming Hanukkah.
ISBN 0-525-46969-9
[1. Hanukkah—Fiction. 2. Jews—Poland—Fiction.
3. Chelm (Lublin, Poland)—Fiction.] I. Schindler, S. D., ill. II. Title.
PZ7.K83565Co 2004
[E]—dc22 2003023632

Published in the United States by Dutton Children's Books,
a division of Penguin Young Readers Group
345 Hudson Street, New York, New York 10014
www.penguin.com

Designed by Tim Hall · Manufactured in China
First Edition
1 3 5 7 9 10 8 6 4 2

To my wondrous wife, Mikki, who was both wise and foolish enough to marry a fool,
and who has inspired this fool with her humor and wisdom

—J.K.

To Mistress Booktender, Ellen Mager

—S.D.S.

There once was a town called Chelm. To a stranger passing through, it might look like any other village. It had the usual number of cottages, barns, and inns, as well as a synagogue at the edge of the town square. Chelm was a simple town. What made it unusual were the people. They were simple, too. So simple, in fact, that some might even call them fools.

One year the Rabbi of Chelm went away on a trip. No one knew where he had gone or when he would be back. Some said he was on a mission to the Holy Land. Some said he was visiting his brother in the Big City. Still others said he was just out for a walk.

It just so happened that Hanukkah was fast approaching. The villagers of Chelm had celebrated Hanukkah every year, but always with the Rabbi. Now that the Rabbi was away, they could not remember how to observe the holiday. So the wise men of Chelm held a meeting, and after many hours of discussion, they decided to send someone to the neighboring town to find out what must be done. They chose Yossel, a likable soul, and he set out for Tevka, only half a day's travel away.

After two days, Yossel began to think he might be going in the wrong direction (which, of course, he was). He stopped by a brook to let his horse drink. "Bubkes," he said to his horse, "should I turn around and go back or continue on?" He had once heard that the shortest route to a place was a straight line. "Since the road is always in front of me," he reasoned, "I must be going the shortest way." So he made the decision to travel on.

The next day he came upon the largest town he had ever seen. "This is amazing, Bubkes!" he said to his horse. "It seems almost a miracle that Tevka should have grown so big! Don't you think?" Bubkes didn't answer but rolled his eyes (because even a horse knew that this was not Tevka, but the Big City).

He rode into the city, his eyes wide at the amazing sights all around him. The buildings were made not of wood and thatch and rough stone, but of brick and marble. The streets were not uneven and dusty, but paved with cobblestones. He saw more people than he thought lived in the whole world, wearing fine silks, soft wools, and warm cozy hats, and speaking languages he had never heard. These must be very smart people indeed! Surely they would know how to celebrate Hanukkah.

He came upon a park, where people were very busy. He could see they were happy and excited. He strode up to a large, friendly-looking fellow.

"Excuse me, sir," said Yossel, "but may I ask what are you doing?"

"Doing? Why, preparing to celebrate the holidays, that's what I'm doing. That's what we're all doing!" He looked at Yossel. "You're not from around here, are you, my friend?"

"No, sir, I'm not. I'm from Chelm, and I've come to learn how to celebrate the coming holiday."

The man clapped Yossel on the shoulder. "Then you've come to the right place!"

The man led Yossel around the park. Yossel saw a woman hanging candies and cookies from a tree. He didn't remember doing that during Hanukkah, but he thought it would be very handy if someone was hungry and needed a tasty snack.

He saw a group of children stringing popcorn and berries into chains. He didn't remember doing that, either. Maybe they used the chains when they wanted to play a game of jump rope.

They came to a great tree, decorated with glass balls, ribbons, and a large star on top. Yossel figured out that because the glass balls were so fragile, hanging them in the tree would keep them safe. The ribbons reminded children not to climb the tree, and the star made a nice place for birds to sit.

Yossel also noticed that there were candles everywhere. He seemed to remember candles . . . but why?

"Isn't it beautiful?" the man said to Yossel. "The festivities continue for several days, so we use lots of candles to make everything bright and merry."

Now Yossel knew he had come to the right place. He recalled lighting candles, and the holiday lasting for several days.

"It's the Festival of Lights. . . . I remember," said Yossel.

"Well," said the man, "I suppose you could call it that, though the children probably think of it as the Festival of Presents. As for me, it's certainly the Festival of Food!" He patted his large belly. "And of course," he added with a wink, "it's always the Festival of the Fat Man!"

"Fat man?" asked Yossel.

"Why, of course! It wouldn't be complete without the fat man to make all the children happy. This year I get to wear the velvet suit and beard."

Yossel was very happy that he had found out how to celebrate Hanukkah. The people of Chelm would be so pleased! He thanked the man and ran back to his wagon. "There now, Bubkes," he said to his horse, "did you have a good rest? I hope so, because now we must go back to Chelm with our wonderful news!"

Several days later, Yossel told the elders all he had learned. Finally, out of breath, he said, "It's called the Festival of Lights. That's what the man said, I remember."

"Yes," said one elder. "The Festival of Lights. I remember that, too!"

"No, no, no," interrupted another elder. "I clearly remember it as the Festival WITH Lights!"

"Nonsense," said a third elder. "It is most certainly THE Festival that HAS Lights!"

They argued for so long that Yossel had a headache from all the shouting.

"But what about the rest? Trees? Fat men? I don't remember any of that!" said the first elder.

"I remember it all quite clearly!" said the second. "Don't you?" he asked the third.

"Remember what?" he said.

"What Yossel has told us?"

"Who's Yossel?" said the third elder, now very confused. "Is he the man from Tevka?"

"No, you yutz! *This* is Yossel!" the first elder said, pointing.

"Hello, Yossel," said the confused elder. "I didn't know you were from Tevka."

The first elder interrupted. "About the holiday . . . maybe what we don't remember are newer customs, and since Tevka is so modern and newfangled, perhaps we should practice these customs as well!" So it was decided. The village would prepare for the holidays as Yossel had described.

Some villagers cut down a large tree and brought it to the town square

while others prepared special treats for the festivities.

Children attached huge matzo balls, wooden dreidels, and shiny menorahs to colorful string and hung them from the tree. Candles were carefully placed on all the branches.

Shmuel the butcher was chosen to be the fat man, for he had the largest stomach in Chelm and he already had a beard. Mendel the tailor made the velvet suit.

Soon they were ready for the holiday.

Just before sundown, the people of Chelm assembled in the town square.

"Let the celebration begin," the elders announced. The villagers cheered, but soon they began murmuring: *What comes next?*

"What comes next, Yossel?" shouted one of the elders.

Yossel gulped. He realized he had never asked the man in Tevka what came next. Everything was silent, except for the loud clacking of Yossel's knees knocking together.

Then a perfectly logical answer came to Yossel. "The next thing is next!" he cried. The elders scratched their heads.

"Yes," sighed the first elder, "but what *is* the next thing?!"

Yossel, feeling a bit faint, yelled out the only thing he could think of: "It's time for the fat man!"

The elders agreed. "Bring out the fat man!" they echoed.

Out came Shmuel the butcher, dressed in a blue velvet suit with white fur trim and a matching yarmulke on his head.

"Here he is, good people of Chelm," the tallest elder announced. "It wouldn't be Hanukkah without . . ." Then he stopped, because he didn't know the name of the character in front of him. But Shmuel had solved the problem. When he was trying on his suit, he had come up with the perfect name. "It's me! Hanukkah Hershel!" he shouted. "*Oy! Oy! Oy!* Happy Hanukkah!"

The people laughed and immediately began to sing a Hanukkah Hershel song. But since there wasn't any Hanukkah Hershel song, each made up his own tune and words until it sounded like everyone had a stomachache. Finally, a small boy named Chaim spoke up. "Wait!" he yelled. "This isn't right."

The elders looked shocked. "What do you mean?" one cried.

"Well," the boy said, "I don't remember ever seeing Hanukkah Hershel before. Do you?"

"Uh . . ." The elders looked worried. Then one pointed his finger at the boy. "Ah, but what about our glorious tree? Surely you remember that?"

"Nope," said Chaim simply.

The elders, the *wise men* of Chelm, were suddenly busy inspecting their own feet. The villagers stopped celebrating. They looked around and knew that the boy was right. They had never seen any Hanukkah Hershel before. And surely, if they had decorated a tree like this in the past, someone would have remembered. But Yossel had told them that other people did these things. And why shouldn't they celebrate the way others did? Still, now it seemed like this wasn't even Hanukkah at all.

That's when they heard a cry from down the road.

"Oy! Oy! Oy!" For a moment they thought it was Hanukkah Hershel again, but he was in front of them, not behind them. The villagers bumped into each other as they turned toward the voice. It was the Rabbi, back from his trip.

"Oy! Oy! Oy! I thought I would be late. Is everybody ready to celebrate Hanukkah!?"

"Of course, Rabbi," said the shortest elder. "Just look around!"

The Rabbi was amazed at the sight of the decorated tree and of Shmuel in his blue velvet suit.

"This is all very interesting, my friends. Tell me, who instructed you in preparing for the holiday in such a . . . creative way?"

All eyes turned to Yossel, who hardly noticed because he was too busy fainting. One of the women poured some cold beet soup on his head to revive him, and the Rabbi helped him to his feet.

"Not to worry, Yossel. You may have gotten things a bit confused, but the confusion in your head is small compared to the wisdom in your heart."

He patted Yossel on the back to make him feel better. "So," said the Rabbi, "now let us all celebrate with our own traditions, shall we? Gather round and I shall tell you the story of Hanukkah."

"Many years ago, the Temple of Jerusalem was captured by an evil king, Antiochus, who thought everybody should believe what he believed. He made a law that if Jews practiced their religion, they would be killed. A small band of rebels named the Maccabees (which means 'hammers') fought Antiochus's army and recaptured the Temple. Now, the Temple had been defiled, so they began to clean up and set things right. They found only one small jar of holy oil to light the Temple menorah—enough to keep it lit for perhaps one day. But it was all they had until more could be pressed. So they used the oil, and, miracle of miracles, the flames of the Temple menorah burned brightly for eight days. Eight days! Long enough to press more oil. We celebrate Hanukkah to remember this miracle. That is why our *Hanukkiah*, our special Hanukkah menorah, has nine flames—one for each day the miraculous oil burned and one that is used to light all the others. And that is why we sometimes call this joyous holiday the Festival of Lights!"

"The Festival of Lights!" the villagers cheered.

"Ah!" said one elder very loudly. "The Festival of Lights! I knew it!"

"What? You knew it? I told *you! I* knew it!" said another even louder.

"Whew!" was all Yossel said, very softly, because at least he had gotten one thing right.

With a wave of his hand, the Rabbi reached into his bag and took out the *Hanukkiah*, with two of the candles in place. He set it on the table and lit the center candle. Then, with that candle, he lit the other and recited the Hanukkah blessings.

So the people of Chelm ate and sang and played games and gave gifts and had the best Hanukkah they'd ever had. From that day forward, it was said that the people of Chelm always remembered how to keep Hanukkah. It was said that theirs was the best festival in all the old country, year after year.

And Shmuel did not have to give up his blue velvet suit. He kept it in his closet and put it on every year to remind himself and everyone else of their foolishness—of the year Chelm had a very special Hanukkah.